About This Book

Title: *Pet Tricks*

Step: 2

Word Count: 350

Skills in Focus: final blends

Tricky Words: after, come, fish, good, Mr. Ash, other, school, show, together

Ideas For Using This Book

Before Reading:
- **Comprehension:** Look at the title and cover image together. Ask the readers to make a prediction.
- **Accuracy:** Practice the tricky words listed on Page 1.
- **Phonemic Awareness:** Explain to the readers that a blend is two consonants together that each make a sound. Preview story words containing final blends, beginning with *best*. Segment the sounds slowly and have the students call out the word. Offer other examples that will appear in the book: *hand*, *tank*, *desk*, calling attention to each final blend.

During Reading:
- Have the students point under each word as they read it.
- **Decoding:** If stuck on a word, help readers say each sound and blend it together smoothly.
- **Comprehension:** Invite students to add to or change their predictions from before reading.

After Reading:
Discuss the book. Some ideas for questions:
- Discuss the characters. Who are the pet owners? Their pets?
- What trick was each pet able to do?
- What does Ben say to Rex after each pet's trick? What does Rex repeat?
- How did Ben feel when Rex wouldn't get the ball? Explain how you know.

Pet Tricks

Text by Leanna Koch

Educational Content by
Kristen Cowen

Illustrated by
Mike Byrne

PICTURE WINDOW BOOKS
a capstone imprint

Pam, Ben, Max, and Sam are best pals. Pam has Jax the rat. Ben has Rex the dog.

Sam has Dot the cat. Max has Fran the fish. The friends play with their pets together.

It is pet day at the kids' school.

"Do you want to come to class?"
Ben asks Rex.

Rex pants and wags.

The rest of the pets come too.
Sam pets Dot. Jax sits on Pam's
hand. Max has Fran in her tank.

"Pet Day is the best!" the kids yell.

"Get a quick rest," Ben tells Rex.
"We can show the class your
tricks after the test."

Ben sits at his desk. He
does his best on the test.

At last, Mr. Ash tells the class
it is time to get the pets.

Max stands at the desk with
Fran's tank. "Fran can swim fast
and jump," Max tells the class.

"Fran is fast, but your tricks are the best," Ben tells Rex.

Rex wags and pants.

Dot sits on the desk by her best pal Sam. "Dot is a soft cat. Dot likes pats on the back," Sam tells the class.

"Dot is soft and fun to pet, but your tricks are the best," Ben tells Rex.

Rex wags and pants.

Jax sits on Pam's hand. "Jax
is a big help," Pam tells the
class. "When I mop, Jax dusts."

"Jax is a good rat, but your tricks are the best," Ben tells Rex.

Rex wags and pants.

Rex sits by Ben at Mr. Ash's desk.
"Rex is the best dog," Ben tells
the class. "Rex has lots of tricks."

At last, Ben gets to show Rex's tricks to his class.

"Get it!" Ben tells Rex.

Rex just wags and pants.

"Don't just sit by the
desk!" Ben huffs at Rex.

Rex winks.

Ben is upset.

"Let's get a snack!" Mr. Ash
tells the class.

Rex runs past the desks.

Rex runs fast.

Rex picks up Ben's bag.

"Good job!" Ben tells Rex.
"You got me a snack!"

"That is a good trick!"
Mr. Ash says.

"Yes," says Ben. "Rex is
the best dog."

More Ideas:

Phonemic Awareness Activity

Practicing Final Blends:
Tell the readers you will say two words with a final blend. They must listen and decide if the words have the same ending blend. If the blends are the same, tell students to touch the top of their head. If the blends are different, tell students to cross their arms (forming an X) over their chest. Discuss the blends in each pair of words.

Suggested words: *rest/dust*; *pant/desk*; *test/past*; *jump/help*; *hand/stand*

Extended Learning Activity

Comic Strip Retell
Retell the important parts of the story in a comic strip format! Discuss the important events in the order they happened. What happened at the beginning? Middle? End? Separate a sheet of paper into the desired number of sections. Draw pictures to show key events from the story in sequence. Add speech bubbles to include the characters' thoughts and/or words.

Published by Picture Window Books,
an imprint of Capstone
1710 Roe Crest Drive,
North Mankato, Minnesota 56003
capstonepub.com

Pet Tricks was originally published as
The Best Trick, copyright 2011 by Picture Window Books.

Library of Congress Cataloging-in-Publication Data is available
on the Library of Congress website.

ISBN: 9780756595753 (hardback)
ISBN: 9780756585945 (paperback)
ISBN: 9780756590352 (eBook PDF)

Printed and bound in the USA. 5757